# The Mollops

Davis McAlonan

Published by S L Davies, 2022.

This is a work of fiction. Similarities to real people, places, or events are entirely coincidental.

THE MOLLOPS

**First edition. September 13, 2022.**



ISBN: 979-8215046869

Written by Davis McAlonan.

# Table of Contents

# Chapter One

The air was light and had a sweet smell of jacaranda; the sun wasn't hot yet, which was a nice change. Although the grass really could have done with a mow, I had been wondering what the boys had done with the cow as I sat sipping my first cup of coffee for the morning, stretched out on the back patio. The cockatoo's fought in the gum trees in the back paddock and the kangaroo's nibbled away at my rose buds. It was truly beautiful out in Lambert, a town with only seventy-five people, a pub, a school and a church, I think the pub came first and then the church.

"MUM"

I near spat my coffee all over the place as a scream broke the silence of the country air. I knew the scream came from John, my youngest, before I saw him tearing up the back yard, leaping over the gate that separated the sheep from my vegie patch and up on the back porch, his face white with terror.

"Matt's chasing me with a tiger snake, he reckons if I don't play footy with 'im he is gonna make the bugger bite me".

Sighing I stood up and roared, "Matthew Bartholomew James Mollop, put that damned snake down and stop threatening to use it as a weapon on your brother, he doesn't have to play footy with yer if he doesn't want to".

Sheepishly I saw Matt come out from behind the eucalyptus tree and place the five-foot tiger snake down on the ground, which slithered away into the scrub. Matt sauntered up the backyard slowly, poking his tongue out at John as he walked past, John still hid behind my back in fear.

"Oh John the bloody snake's gone now, you can stop hiding"

"He was gonna bite me with it" he whined

"No he wasn't, he was just threating because he knows you give a good reaction, remember he didn't cut your leg off with the axe when he threated to, he didn't shoot you in the bum when he threatened to, he just does it because you scream" I sighed.

This was always happening, they picked on John all the time because he was just so gullible, must have got that from his father's side of the family.

"Na this time he really would 'ave mum" he said waltzing off into the house.

"You wait until I take your dog hunting I'm gonna kick it in the nuts" I heard Matt mutter quietly.

"Matthew" I growled, before John had a chance to come back out to dob.

Those are two of my children, there is an older son too. His name is Michael, or Blue, as he is known in these parts, due to his carrot red hair. He spends most of his time fixing the car, making it better he says, or riding his motorbike. We don't see him too often, usually he is up before the sparrow has a chance to have its first fart of the day and in bed not long after dinner. He says a man has to have a good night's rest and get the best out of the whole day. Just like his father I say.

# Chapter Two

You now have been introduced to my three boys, but let me tell you a bit more about the town of Lambert; you see it's an interesting town, a town not quite like any other. As I have already said there are only about seventy five people, most of which are all related somehow, either by marriage or blood.

So where do we start, well let's start at the top, the mayor, we may be a small town and not much happens around here but we have a mayor, he is a top bloke too I might say. His name is Bill.

He once told us how he went hunting one sunny afternoon and after he slung his shotgun over his shoulder he shot himself in the leg. They never could find the bullet until one mysterious day, his stomach started hurting really bad. He had never felt pain like it before. He thought maybe it was his wife Beryl's cooking from that evening; she wasn't the greatest of cooks. Suddenly he knew he had to race to the toilet, he was going to lose his guts, in his words. But as he stood up and turned to put his paper on the chair, it was too late. He let rip with the biggest, loudest fart that he had ever heard. His stomach began to ease, so he decided to forgo the toilet trip and sit to enjoy the rest of his paper, but as he turned he saw his beloved mongrel dog lying in a pool of blood, dead on the ground. Beryl came running at the sound of the fart; obviously she had never heard one quite that loud before either. They both stood looking down at Mac, the dog, she looked up at Bill.

"Well darl, I think we found the bullet".

Mayor Bill also has a unique way of keeping kids in school, before we had a mayor, the kids were unruly and they were up to all sorts of mischief. But Mayor Bill was our hero, with a shining axe. Yes that's what I said. He chases the kids into school with an axe, threating to cut off their toes and fingers if they didn't get on in there, has worked every time. Until we had a family make one of those sea changes or in this case a tree change, cause there's no ocean for miles, anyway they made the change as city folks are fond of doing. This kid just didn't want to do anything, he didn't heed the warnings of other kids and one day Mayor Bill just happened to be down getting a hamburger from the pub and there was this city kid, bold as a brass pair of balls smiling cheekily at old Bill.

"Do I need to get me axe out boy and cut yer toes off?" Bill said loudly.

"Yup I reckon ya do" the boy replied with a smug look on his face.

The pub went deadly silent, never before had any kid dared to challenge Bill on his threat before. Well I don't think I need to go into too many details about what happened next, let's just say that this kid now walks with a permanent limp and has never left school even though he's now forty-five years old.

# Chapter Three

Bill makes a great mayor and I don't reckon there would be anyone willing to take over his job, but someone who is also a top person in Lambert is the publican and his wife, Joe and Bernie.

They've owned the pub forever. They came here with a dream in mind, to build the most popular pub in the North West region of Victoria. And I reckon they have just about darn well done it too. Every Friday night you can be guaranteed that the shearers will drive the hundred kilometres or so to get to our little watering hole, not just for the cold beer on tap but for the biggest and freshest steak around. Bernie is an awesome cook; she is famous around here for her steaks, burgers and chips, with eggs on the side. Just about every truckie that rolls on through these parts stops in for a shower, steak and a chin wag. But that's not the only thing Bernie is famous for.

You see, how do I put it? Bernie is a, well a fridge with arms and legs. She stands at five feet ten, boobs the size of mountains and arms, well let's just say she has the whole New Testament tattooed on one arm and it fits! She may be big, but she loves Joe endlessly. He's a big bloke too, but skinny as a rake, she feeds him up but he never seems to put on weight, there's rumours as to why that is, but I don't want to get into those, keep it clean I reckon.

Anyway, the pub is a bit of a rowdy place, especially around the time of shearing, when all the young bucks come in to have a drink and watch the Friday night entertainment. And quite often than not there will always be a fight or two. Most of the shearers are reasonable boys, they will take it outside, but every now and then we get a new shearer who studied shearing at one of them Uni's and he'll get a bit too much grog in his belly and want to punch something. Well this happened one evening not too far back actually.

The kid was only about eighteen I reckon, fresh faced thing he was, bit cocky as all the city one's seem to be. And sure enough Becky, the young bar maid, she is old Macca's daughter, she is a lovely little thing, she's saving to move to the city and get herself a career as a teacher or nurse or something. Anyway, Becky had stopped serving this kid because he had, had too much to drink. And as usual they don't like it when they stopped getting served and they begin to look for trouble. Well I tell you this night he found it. Smithy happened to be in the bar. He is about six foot five tall and just as wide and always happy to lay down a few city blokes.

So sure enough this city kid slams down his glass and slurs something about Smithy's mum. There are just a few things that you don't do in the country, knock off a bloke's hat, bag out his dog and slander his mum. And this kid broke one of the country commandments. So Smithy stands up, Becky yells out to Bernie that there is about to be a punch on. The city kid stands looking directly at Smithy's chest. Smithy picks him up by the collar of his shirt and looks deep in his eye.

"What'd yer say about me ma?" he growls.

"I said she likes it when I..." The city kid didn't get to finish, as he suddenly had to spit out his teeth onto the floor.

Smithy reached down to pick him off the floor to go in for the kill. When suddenly that big six foot five oaf was screaming like a girl. The pub spun to see what had happened and there Bernie stood behind him, Smithy's undies firmly in her hand.

"I've told you a hundred times before Smithy, you wanna fight, you bloody well take it outside, not in me pub" she growled through gritted teeth, marching him, undies still in hand, out the glass door.

The city kid was still sitting on the floor dazed out of his brain, missing his front teeth and blood on his chin.

"Get up ya bloody sook, he didn't hit ya that hard" Bernie said as she walked past him to get some ice out of the icebox.

Slowly he clambered back onto his stool, head down and his face red with embarrassment.

"Mate that was some hit ya took and to say that about his ma, mate not too many blokes survive that, well down fella" said one of the truckies.

"Yeah let us buy ya round. Becky a strong whiskey for the kid 'ere". Macca called from the end of the bar.

After that the night went smoothly and Smithy never fought inside the pub again. He always carried the cocky young fella's out that back of the pub to knock their teeth in. There they would be Sunday morning, singing the hymns with a lisp.

# Chapter Four

Speaking of lisps, Bernie had a shocking lisp when she first came to Lambert; you see Bernie didn't have any teeth. She has many a tale about how she lost them; sometimes it will be in a fight, other times it will be in a car accident. The latest one I heard her tell was that a kangaroo was eating her vegies and she went to shoo it away and it kicked her fair square in the teeth knocking them straight out of her mouth. The stories get bigger as quickly as her belly grows.

But she has a lovely set of teeth now, they don't fit properly. But I guess beggars can't be choosers. Lambert doesn't have a dentist. In fact that nearest one is in Mildura, which is almost one hundred and seventy kilometres away. But late one evening, Bernie was cleaning up after the Friday night show and something caught her eye on the sticky floor, hidden below a table that sat up against the stage.

Bernie ambled her way down onto her knee's crouching low below the table, the smell of old cigarette smoke and stale beer hitting her nostrils, she reached under the table, touching the floor feeling for the loot that had caught her sharp eye. Touching a cigarette butt, a piece of paper, a bottle top and suddenly her hand landed on it, clasping it tight in her fat hand, she brought it up to her face for a closer inspection, grinning a toothless grin.

Bernie stood quickly and went to the kettle, boiling the water, impatient to test out her new loot. She reached up high, looking for a bowl.

"Joe" she screeched "Bring us a bowl, I found meself some teef".

Joe came down the stairs from their apartment, bowl in hand. Bernie put the teeth in the bowl, pouring the boiled water over the top. Joe looked on, uninterested.

"Where'd ya find 'em luv?" he asked looking down at her.

"They were just under the table over there, I reckon one of the city folk musta left 'em there, too excited over the entertainment, he lost 'is teef" she laughed, as her excitement mounted.

For too long Bernie had been tootles, she felt unattractive, but Mildura was too far to go to see the denture clinic and they cost so much money that she couldn't bring herself to buy them. Fifteen minutes later, Bernie went to the drawer under the sink in the bar and fetched out a pair of tongs, she carefully pulled the false teeth out of the bowl and ran them under cold water in the sink. With her left hand she felt them to make sure the temperature was cool enough. When Bernie was satisfied, she slowly put them in her mouth. Clicking her tongue on the top, smiling, opening and shutting her mouth, getting the feel that she had thought she had forgotten; the feeling of a full mouth of teeth.

Bernie turned and looked at Joe who was busy cleaning the bowl and putting the kettle away. She smiled at him, the biggest grin she could muster. She felt her teeth slip down a bit and clicked them back into place with her tongue.

"Oh luv they look beautiful, just like when ya were eighteen" Joe swooned.

Bernie's face flushed, she felt beautiful again. She now had teeth; she would smile all the time, showing off her new pearly whites. Joe came to her and wrapped his skinny arms around her waist.

"Come on luv, all this can wait, let's go to bed and 'ave a cuddle" Joe said, as he nuzzled into her ample breast.

Her smile was as wide as a Cheshire cat as she skipped up the steps, Joes hand firmly in hers and giggles of excitement escaping her lips.

# Chapter Five

But thinking about Friday nights, the Friday night entertainment is very popular around here. I reckon it's just because there isn't really anything better to do. We only have two channels of TV and even then they are full of static and turn off by six in the evening. So Friday nights at the pub are the best thing we have to do.

I bet you are wondering what the entertainment is that I have been raving about. Well I guess you could say it is kind of like a stripper, kind of like a dancer and kind of like a singer. Ok so well you see, I have a brother, his name is Morrie and he is a lovely guy. And well how do I say this, he is, well you know one of them guys that likes to dress as women. My parents were a bit shocked when he first told them, but after a little while they got used to it. Morrie is just Morrie, in a dress. And as you have probably gathered he is our Friday night entertainment.

Morrie likes to go by the name of Diva Davina. He has old Mrs Miller make is sequined dresses, she is a retired tap dancer, who still thinks she's in the twenties, but she can sew up a storm. So there he is every Friday night on the creaky old stage of the pub, the lights down low, a blue glow coming from the centre of the stage, the smoke machine coughing out smoke into the audience.

The music slowly begins an instrumental version of Celine Dion's "My heart will go on", a silhouetted figure stands on the stage, hand raised high in the sky holding a fan of feathers.

Suddenly with a bright red spark the music switches into Dolly Parton's "nine to five" and there stands Diva Davina, in a sequined tight fitting green dress, breasts that put Bernie's to shame, a wig that I'm sure is about three feet tall and ratty looking, nails long and red, lipstick to match and dark blue eye shadow. Diva struts down the stage mouthing to the words to "nine to five" shaking her breasts and flirting with the drunken shearers, who wolf whistle and cheer as she swings her legs high in the sky and kicks her stilettos into the audience.

The shearers leap over one another to catch the shoes and sniff them and pretend to faint in erotic pleasure. Diva will then slowly strip down to a small one piece of lingerie, bending over and peeking through her legs, winking at the men, who are considerably more drunk as the show goes on. Finally the end draws near and Diva sits on the edge of the stage, crossing her legs seductively and mouths the words to Jennifer Rush's "Power of love". She wipes a tear from her eye and reaches into the crowd. Bernie comes forward, red plastic roses in hand. Diva takes the roses and kisses Bernie on the cheek and thanks her with an exaggerated bow. She turns and saunters up the stage, swaying her hips. As the song draws to its end, Diva turns back to the men, who have all fallen silent and are sipping quietly on their beer and winks, blowing them a kiss as she walks off the stage as the lights dim into darkness.

When the lights come back on, Bernie is standing on the stage.

"Last call for drinks fella's so get a move on" she barks into the microphone, as shearers begin to stand and move on their way back to the bar and pool tables.

Morrie is in the back room, surrounded by a mirror, sequined dresses and brooms.

"Oh wasn't that an excellent show, it was the best one yet" he exclaims.

"It was the same as it always is Morrie" I sigh.

"No, no, no this time I strutted rather than wiggled, you mean you didn't notice?"

I couldn't say I did, the truth was that I thought Morrie's shows were getting a bit boring, it was entertaining at the start but he did the same songs every week. However, he would be hurt if I didn't show up every week.

"I'm thinking about taking it on the road to Melbourne, what do you think?" he spun in his stool, his wig removed and hair in a stocking.

"Yeah ya could do that I suppose" I said poking through the endless supply of sequined dresses.

# Chapter Six

It wouldn't be like he didn't have anywhere to go in Melbourne; our sister now lives there with her big shot lawyer husband and daughters. She went and got herself a career, apparently Lambert was suffocating her. I personally couldn't see the attraction of the city, with all those people that look like ants, filing in and out of trains and buildings all day long.

The smog that chokes you, if you ask me the city is more suffocating that the country. But Sharon, that's me sister, she says she would never come back to Lambert, even if someone paid her to. Her husband Max works for a law firm in the city and they live in a big house in Balwyn, apparently they even have a pool and a spa. Me, I personally prefer to just go for a dip in the dam out the back paddock, yeah there are a few leaches and yabbies, but nothing that can't be flicked off. I asked her what the point of swimming in a pool full of chlorine is; she reckons it's better because it's cleaner. I don't see the point, still got flies buzzing around your head in Balwyn.

Their daughters Lauren and Janelle are twenty-one and fifteen; they are snot nosed brats if you ask me. All about look what I've got, have you got a big screen telly; I need one of them designer bags. Don't see the point of those either, nothing that a Safeway's bag can't carry. Janelle came up to visit one weekend not that long back, she was hopeless, too busy worrying about her nails to be of any use. Took her in the back of the ute to feed the sheep, she squealed because there was a bloody spider in the hay, well what the hell did she expect there to be, roses and perfume? She complained constantly about how the pig stinks, well it swims in its own turds it's not going to smell like Calvin Klein is it? To be honest I was glad to see the back of her.

The shearers thought she was a bit of alright. They wanted to take her out, but those boys only have one thing on their mind and be buggered if I was gonna send my niece home with pups in her gut. It ended up being more of a headache shooing away the shearers away who were sniffing around like Janelle was a dog on heat. Not that she seemed to mind the attention, but I reckon Pete got a hell of a lot greyer after that weekend. He reckons it's worse cause he knew what the shearers were thinking.

# Chapter Seven

Anyway, I mentioned the ute before; it's a great piece of work, there is none like it in the world. Ours in completely unique. As I said way up there at the start, my eldest boy Michael or Blue as we often call him, on account of his red hair, well he is a bit of a whiz with a spanner. Well as I said he gets up really early, usually he's pretty good and goes and feeds Fanny Mabel, the cow, the lawn really needs a mow. But once he's finished giving her a bit of loosen and some left over bread, he's off to the shed to tinker.

One Sunday morning, I got up as usual six am on the dot; I rolled onto my side and peeked out through the crack in the curtains to see a beautiful clear blue sky. I lay there watching the dust bunny's do their dance in the flinting light; enjoying the warmth of the sun that was just beginning to poke its head up over the mountains. As I stood up I could see the dust bunny's begin to soar around my head frantically, trying to regain their peaceful pattern.

I stumbled my way out to the toilet, dying for a wee. Sitting on the outhouse, looking at the magazine pictures of forties pin up girls that were glued to the wall. Listening to the splash hitting the tin edges of the dunny can. When suddenly a movement caught my eye. At first I thought it was a snake, but I knew it was too early for them to be out and about.

"Is that you Rusty?" I called to our red Kelpie who liked to get up early in the morning, to catch rabbits and bring them home for show and tell.

"Na mum it's me, just fixin' the ute, makin' it betta" Blue called out to me.

I shuffled my way back to the kitchen for my morning coffee and a bit of toast, before getting ready for church. Standing up against the hardwood kitchen bench, wiping the sleep out of my eyes, I watched Blue walk out of the tractor shed with the axel of the tractor in hand. I laughed, thinking he was trying to fix the old tractor that broke down a few months ago. Probably making it better. I heard the pop of the kettle button let me know it was ready and could smell the condensation from the boiled water behind me. At the same time I heard the muffled sounds of Matt and John moving their way down the hallway.

"Hey Ma I can't find me Sundy clothes" John whined.

He is our preacher in the making, he loves church that boy, would probably live there if he could.

"Have you checked your cupboard?" I asked sleepily.

That's the problem with boys; you have to do the thinking for them. Just like his father. I could hear a cheer as he obviously found his clothes in the cupboard as I said. Matt was already sitting on the play station as I could hear the sounds of guns or race cars; I don't know they all sound the same to me.

"Matt come and make breakfast, won't be long and you'll be getting ready for church" I called.

"Mornin' luv, how'd ya sleep?" I felt the soft kiss on the top of my head and the familiar whiskers of my husband.

He is a livestock truckie, pretty well known here, when there is a drought he'll move the stock for the neighbours for free. Top bloke is my Pete. I looked up at him and smiled as he ran his hand along my shoulder on his way out the back door to the outhouse.

"Hey luv, what's Blue up to?" I heard him yell back through the door.

"Fixin' the tractor I think" I yelled back. "Matthew get yer damned breakfast will ya; yer still gotta have a shower yet"

I could hear Matt mumble something about always going to church and throw the controller down, before stomping into the kitchen. He crashed open the cupboard door and pulled out a bowl as nosily as possible, just to let me know he was annoyed. I watched him as he swung the pantry door near off its hinges to grab out the weetbix box. He turned to see if I was still watching him, I poked my tongue out and caught him give a little smile, but soon covered it up with a frown, just to let me know I wasn't yet forgiven.

I went for my shower and got dressed in my Sunday dress, it is about the only time I wear a dress, apart from Sharon's wedding, Sunday is the only day. And then at Sharon's wedding I had to borrow one of Morrie's sequined gowns, we were in the middle of a drought and didn't have the money to go to Mildura to buy a new one. I felt like a right idiot, but my mum reckoned I looked alright. I don't think Max's family thought so. Guess they're just not used to country folk. Different breed I reckon. Probably should have had Mrs Miller sew on a Versace tag on it and I might have fit in.

By the time I got out of the shower, Blue was standing in the kitchen in his Sunday clothes, hair brushed and face cleaned, eating a piece of toast. It was times like these that I realised what a handsome son I had. He stood at just a little over six feet tall, with a light tan, red wild hair and bright blue eyes. I patted his back and gave him a bit of a squeeze.

"Get the tractor fixed luv?" I asked looking up at him.

"Yeah sorta" he mumbled with a mouthful of toast.

"Ya ready to go luv?" I turned to see Pete standing in the doorway, his black suit a little too short in the arms. He always looked so uncomfortable in his suit, but I guess so did all the farmers, shearers and truckies every Sunday. The only ones that ever looked suave were the city folk coming for a visit.

I nodded and grabbed my handbag and old black leather tattered bible from off the small wooden table that Pete had made me when we first got married. The boys were all lagging behind, John and Matt, planning what prank they would play on the preacher Rev. James this week.

"No pranks, I want a nice service, got it?" I snapped, spinning on my heel to look at them.

They sullenly nodded and walked forward, but it wasn't long before I could hear them whispering the prank instead. And that was when I saw it. I had rounded the corner of the shed and there sat my ute, rusty and paint flaking. But there was something different about it. Instead of my ute being normal size, there it sat on two tractor axles and four tractor wheels.

"Whoa that is slammin'" yelled Matt.

I was speechless.

"Ma, shut ya mouth, yer will catch flies" John giggled.

I turned to look at him and then Blue.

"What'd ya do to me ute luv?" I asked.

"Made it better mum"

"Hmm, how?" I asked a little confused by how making it stand four foot in the air was making it better.

"Well now yer got a tractor and a ute" Blue stated.

I could see his point.

"Flamin' hell, what the hell happened to the ute?" Pete yelled.

"Blue made it better" I said, opening the door that stood above my head.

"Here ya mum" Blue said, putting is hands down and clasping them so I could put my foot in to be boosted up into the seat. As I hoisted myself up, I felt his shoulder on my bum to give me that extra shove.

"I've gotta make a ladder for it yet, ran outta time this mornin'" he called.

I nodded still not sure what to think. Not sure what all the church folk would think when they saw us rolling in with our tractor ute. Pete climbed up in the driver's seat, while Matt, Blue and John made their way into the tray. I heard the engine come alive. Pete giggled the whole way.

"Blue made it better" he would giggle.

As we rolled into the yard of the church, our friends and family stopped and stared. Pete pulled the ute to a stop and opened the door. I saw Blue come around to the passenger door.

"Here ya mum, let me help ya" he said as he reached into the door way and wrapped his arms around my waist and levered me down.

I could hear the giggles and sniggers. Then I heard Pete's loud voice.

"Blue made it better" he boomed and erupted into violent laughter.

He was joined by a chorus of laughter. Blue grew another ten feet with pride. He had made the ute better.

# Chapter Eight

Now I guess I better tell you about Rev. James. He isn't like any other preacher we've had here in Lambert. He is only new here, been here about ten years I reckon. The preacher we had before him, old Rev. Patrick, was a hard drinker, drank himself into kidney failure. Most sermons' he wrote and preached drunk I reckon. Usually we got the gist of things. The kids thought it was funny to count how many times he said Steve instead of Adam and almost fell off the altar. But Rev. James, he is one of those young reverends, the ones that you see on TV all hip and happening. He's not a bad sort.

But I tell ya get him on the footy field and there isn't any God that could stop him. We play AFL here, got our own team, the players change every couple of weeks, because the shearers move onto work up north and the cattle labourers come down for dipping and mustering so we get them on the team. But Rev. James, tough, he is tough as nails.

I'll never forget two years ago it was. We had to beat Tempe to get into the grand final, it was so close and we were only two points ahead. We knew that if Tempe just got one goal we would be done for. So we were depending on a miracle from God Himself and who better to call for that miracle than Rev. James. I remember it was the last quarter, he gathered the boys in a tight circle, arms around one another and he bowed his head, closed his eyes and began to pray.

"Dear Heavenly Father, if you could please see fit, that we can beat the snot out of the blokes from Tempe, we would be much appreciative, thanks. In Jesus name, Amen".

Well we got our miracle that day we beat them by thirty two pints and no injuries. Same couldn't be said for the Tempe blokes. Rev. James broke two noses in a tackle. But we were all mates at the pub afterwards. No losers in the country, only mates that aren't as good.

But he is a top bloke Rev. James. He is great with the kids, between him and Mayor Bill; the kids here are on the straight and narrow. The church set up one of them youth groups. Rev. James reckons they are a big thing in the city, gives the kids something to do. They hold discos and stuff, no drinking there. It's good for the kids, otherwise they get into all sorts of mischief, but Rev. James has been real good keeping the kids busy.

The youth group will often get out and do chores for the old cocky's who are struggling a bit, like painting their sheds or reposting their fences. I remember one year right before old Frank kicked the bucket, he was real sick, he had cancer in all his bones, he was a right trooper, never liked to ask for help. He had been a digger in the First World War, tough bloke, made something out of nothing. But his crops were about to turn bad and he didn't have the energy to bring them in.

So it was Rev. James that organised the youth group to get out there and bring the crops in for him. They borrowed a harvester from old man Peterson and borrowed our tractor ute and got it all in, in a day. Frank died the following week. Poor Mrs Bartlett found him dead in his chair by the front door, his old Kelpie lying there by his side. The Kelpie died not long after, I don't reckon she could cope without him there.

It's always a big thing in Lambert, a death. You know they are going to happen, but you always wish they wouldn't. Everyone turned out to Frank's funeral; the church was splitting at the seams. And then we all slowly followed Bernie in her station wagon, holding Frank's casket, back to his family farm where he lived all his married life with his once beautiful wife Georgia, she died of a heart attack about ten years before Frank. Together they had three children, Eric, he was a good boy and lost his life in Vietnam, broke his mother and father's heart. Georgia was never the same after that.

I wasn't alive when the Vietnam War was on, so I don't remember the day they got the news about Eric. But my mum has told me the story. Eric was the only boy in Lambert to go to the war. He wasn't conscripted he had already joined the army, just after the Korean War, when he turned eighteen. Apparently Georgia was terrified about him going, being in such an isolated town, you don't get a lot of information, not like today with the internet and Facebook. Back then, you waited for the city folk to bring news or what the paper wrote.

Anyway Eric wrote to his mother regularly but then one day the letters stopped. Georgia would wait for the postie every day to bring her a new letter. She started losing weight with worry. She wrote to Eric, but never heard back. It wasn't like she could just ring his mobile phone or Skype him. It was nearing the end of the war and Georgia was sitting on the veranda watching for the postie, when a big black car drove up the dusty road and turned into the driveway. Frank said that he heard Georgia scream before the men had even had a chance to step out of the car. He tried to console her, telling her that it might not be what she thought.

The two men got out of the car and slowly walked towards where Frank and Georgia stood.

"I'm sorry to say but your son has died during action. He died a hero" one man said, reaching forward to touch Georgia on the arm.

Apparently the story goes that Georgia lost it, she screamed at the man and punched the other in the face. Frank reckons it's a good thing they didn't want to cart her off to jail, that they understood it was grief. But for the rest of her days she would sit on that veranda everyday waiting for the postie to bring a letter from Eric. They were never able to recover his body, which is what she held onto. As far as Georgia was concerned if there was no body, there was a possibility he was still alive and just hiding. She often would tell people that she believed he just got scared and ran away and doesn't know the war ended.

Their daughter was Joyce, she's married with a tribe of kids and living in Mildura and their youngest son, Stevie, he now run's the farm, he was the only one living here in Lambert when his dad passed, he was only just eighteen and working as a shearer the day Frank was found on the veranda.

We all stood in the old family farm, dressed in black, the men pulling at the sleeves of their suits, the kids fighting with the flies that buzzed around their heads as they lowered Franks casket into the hole next to his wife's and Eric's plot. Joyce howled, her husband holding her in his arms, handing her a handkerchief. Stevie just stood silent, his face set in determination to keep the farm alive. And to this very day he has done just that. Everyone reckons he is just like his old man. He had a will of steel and a stubborn streak, won't ask for help, even if it meant running himself to death, just as his father did.

The country women's association, run by mum made the scones, cakes and slices that we all ate at the pub, talking about what a great bloke Frank was. It's funny you know, the bloke could have been the coldest, meanest son of a bitch there was, but at his funeral you never hear a bad word spoken about them. It's a good way to be I reckon.

# Chapter Nine

Now speaking of my mum, she's the head of everything. She runs the C.W.A here in Lambert, she is the president of the craft group at the church, she organises the yearly fete and the yearly lamington bake off. There isn't a thing go on that my mum doesn't know about. If someone new moves into town, she is the first to be there on their doorstep with a basket of jams and a welcoming smile. And I can guarantee ya that she will know their whole life story within the first hour. And then in the second hour she spends the time ringing the whole of Lambert to tell them.

All in all she is a pretty great person, my mum. She raised us four kids well. Firm but well. There was always plenty of tucker on the table and well she has put up with me dad for God knows how long and that would be a feat in itself. Let me describe my dad to you. He is a collect-a-holic, he loves little bits and pieces, he has the eye of a magpie for anything shiny and an afternoon Sunday drive isn't a Sunday drive without dad stopping about forty times to pick something up off the side of the road.

My dad mostly spends all of his time in his overflowing shed. It's a little twelve foot by ten foot shed in his backyard, with floor to ceiling wooden shelves that he made himself. On these shelves sit, jars of various sizes, filled with rusty nails, screws, bolts, nuts and bits of metal that could be useful for something. I'll never forget one afternoon; I was only sixteen at the time. And we were on our Sunday afternoon drive in the HQ Holden ute, Betsy her name was, blue and full of rust, as is most of the utes around here, her exhaust pipe was long gone and if you looked through the tray of the ute, you could watch the road go by. It was kind of fun when we watched the road kill go under and we would try to spit globby bits down on top of them.

But here we were this day on our drive, the sun shone, dad with his elbow on the window sill, wind blew all three of the hairs that were left on his head, beside him was my little brother Dale in his booster seat and my mum sitting next to him, holding the bottle that jutted out Dale's mouth, singing loudly to Slim on the radio. In the tray was me, Sharon and Morrie, stretched out on our bellies watching the road through hole in the tray, chatting about what we hoped to get for Christmas. When suddenly dad came to a screeching halt.

I sat up, to be knocked back down onto my stomach as dad slammed Betsey into reverse and started back down the bumpy road. Watching out the back window, as he drove, he found what he was looking for and stomped on the brakes again. He swung the creaky door open and jumped out. Dad let out a victory cry as he stooped down to pick up his treasure. Sharon, Morrie and I all looked over the tray of the ute to see what he had found. And there crumpled in his hand was a bent five cent piece.

As soon as we got home, dad was straight in to his shed to store away his new found treasure in its appropriate jar. Well Christmas came around fast that year and there we sat under the decorated branch of a gum tree, tinsel shining in the light, my mum ran around taking photos. Sharon and Morrie fought over who the makeup was for. Dale chewed on the wrapping paper, his face turned red with the mix of dye and saliva. Dad came and sidled over to me.

"I've made you a special pressie luv" he said, handing me a small square shaped awkwardly wrapped present in gold paper.

I looked up at him to see the look of excitement and nervous anticipation on his face, as I slowly opened it. Inside was a small wooden box; I looked up at him again, as he began to smile. Everyone had stopped what they were doing to watch as I opened the box. I could hear them all gasp as I peeked and saw a small bracelet made with straightened out five cent pieces. I could feel the tears prickle at the back of my eyes. Never had anyone given me something they had made before. I leapt to my feet and wrapped my arms around dad, snuggling him close as mum watched on, a smile grew across her face. He took me by the shoulders and pushed me away slightly and brought the bracelet up.

"Read it" he said, pointing to the different five cent pieces.

On each piece was a different letter, which spelled out the words "I love you forever and a day, love always dad".

I've never lost that bracelet; it has always been kept in the special little box that he made for me, in a bigger box that I keep all my happy memories in. To be honest with you that is the only thing I really remember from that Christmas, except for Dale throwing up all over Nana, from eating too many boiled eggs and turkey.

# Chapter Ten

Nana, oh dear, what a woman. She is famous in Lambert, as is most of the people that live here, being such a small town, there isn't really anyone that we don't know and if we don't them, we soon get to know then, well at least mum does. Nana is my mum's mum. She is senile now, although I reckon she has been senile since she was twelve. You know all the jokes about blondes? Well nana was never blonde, just vague. Everyone took great pleasure in teasing poor nana, especially my pop, who is dead now, rest his soul. I remember driving in his car one day, a Datsun 180b and we rounded the corner and there in front of us was Lambert's cemetery, it's only little but still everyone dies so we need one. And pop pointed out the window, turning in his seat slightly to look at Sharon and I squeezed in the back seat.

"See that kids, that's the dead centre of Lambert" he giggled.

"How do you know it's the dead centre Paddy?" Nana asked, "I mean it might be a little off centre".

Pop burst out laughing, that big loud deep belly laugh. My pop was an Irish man, who came to Australia during the Second World War, with the Australian Army. His name wasn't Patrick or Paddy, yet it was just the Aussie's way of giving him a nickname. He was a big man, with a round squishy belly. A sly sense of humour and plenty of love to give. Nana never asked him to prune her roses, well that's not true, she did once and she ended up with only a single rose left on each bush. The whole town seemed to be heartbroken the day he died. And the funeral was the biggest turnout ever seen in these parts; I reckon even half of Mildura turned up too.

But once my pop passed on, my Nana found herself really lonely and that was when she met Roy. Roy is a strange bloke. The kids have made stories up about him for years, saying he isn't really human, yet some sort of ghost or ghoul. Roy looks a little like a homeless Einstein character, with wild grey hair that sticks out the top of his head like he stuck his finger in a power point. He wears thick glasses that make his eyes look magnified and fishbowl like. He's a tall man and addicted to cake. That man can polish off a Boston bun faster that a starving dog on a rabbit. It's kinda disgusting watching him, bits of cake flying everywhere, icing and coconut smeared across his lips and chin, his eyes a glazed distant stare in them. Makes me shudder just thinking about it, but he seems to make Nana happy, I don't get it, but I guess I don't have to live with the crazy old bugger.

He spends most of his day in the lower rooms of his house, working with all sorts of electrical equipment, used for all sorts of things. Some equipment is used for talking to people, others are for listening to the police, others are used for God knows what, but if you ask the local kids they would tell you they are for dissecting frogs and turning them into a robotic army that is intending to take over the world.

I must admit that when I first heard that my Nana was dating Roy of all people, I was a little worried. No, that's an understatement, I was downright horrified. This man was weird; he spent hours pouring over the local phone book, all three pages of it, memorizing everyone's phone number and address, looking for new people that moved into the neighbourhood. He was just plain scary. I remember the first time that I met him. I had just got home from school and could hear my mum and nana discussing in the kitchen what lamington recipes they were going to try at this year's bake sale. I walked through the front door and came to a screeching halt as I saw sitting on the green velour couch, this man with tracksuit pants, worn at the knees and too short for him, his flannelette shirt tucked in tight, his hair sticking out at all angles, his glasses pushed tight against his face and his fingers running down the list of the white pages, a pad on the other knee as he furiously wrote down various numbers.

I cleared my throat, to get his attention; he looked up at me slightly startled and dropped the white pages on the floor. I could see that it was Mildura's white pages; I gathered it mustn't have been outs, it was far too thick. He stood awkwardly, walking quickly towards me, his hand out, taking mine.

"Ah hello there, you must be Marree's granddaughter," he said peering in close at me, pushing his glasses back up onto his nose.

"Um yeah, I am, um I don't know you" I said, backing up to get some personal space back.

Holding his belly, he laughed loudly.

"Well I'm Roy" he announced.

I heard my mum and nana behind me and I turned looking at them trying to work out who Roy was.

"This is nana's, um friend" mum answered my quizzical look.

I nodded, realising what she meant and then screwing up my face. He was a very different man to my pop. Not like what I had expected at all.

"Yes he is my boyfriend, we are waiting till we make love though" Nana announced proudly, putting her arm around his waist.

"Um thanks for that Nan, I really don't need to know that though" I called back, shuddering at the images that flooded my head as I walked into my room to get changed.

That night Pete had come to pick me up for a date, we were heading off to the pub for the Friday night show, this was before the time of Morrie, and they still had Slim Dusty play there occasionally then. But this time it was one of the local bush poets called Mick Milligan. Anyway, we had, had a bit of rain that week and Pete had parked the ute out the front of our place on the nature strip.

The problem came when we were ready to leave and we realised the ute was bogged. Dad knew what to do; he went running off to the shed, where he came out proudly carrying a big plank of wood to slip under the back wheel of the ute.

"Knew this would come in handy one day" he said grinning.

Pete got into the driver's seat and revved the big V8 engine, while dad quickly slipped the plank of wood under the spinning wheel. Dad and Roy stood at the back, their faces going red, hands on the bumper straining with every push. Mum, Nana and I watched out the window as the car lurched forwards then back, threatening to release its grip on the dirt below, flicking mud up into dad and Roys face. Suddenly the car shot forward, Roy's feet slipped out from underneath him and he hit the dirt face first. We all held our breath, as he didn't move. Pete jumped out the car thinking he had killed him. Nana screamed his name, waddling her way down the front steps. Mum cackled a wild laugh; I stood wondering if I was adopted into this mad family.

Slowly he began to sit up, dad, Pete and Nana stood around him, helping him to his feet, watching him stumble dizzily, as if he was drunk, up the front path and into the front door, he flopped down onto the couch, closing his eyes for a moment. We stood watching, not sure what to do next. He bent down picked up the white pages that was still sitting on the floor where it had fallen when he introduced himself to me and started pouring through it again.

I looked at my mum quizzically. Mum shrugged her shoulders and left to go into the kitchen to prepare the barbecue.

"He's nuts" I heard my dad mumble as he followed my mum.

My Nana sat down next to him looking lovingly up into face, like a teenager with her first boyfriend. I felt a sick feeling in my stomach watching her. Old people love was never my thing, until I became old and now it's my turn to gross out the kids of today. So that was my introduction to Roy, the weirdo that my Nana lives with. I've never really been able to get used to him. I mean in a way I suppose he's alright but his quirks just weird me out. Some things I have learnt about Roy is, that he is a hypochondriac, he likes to lock himself up in his room and he likes to complain about everything. I suppose that might sound like a lot of old people but with Roy I guess, he's just special. There is just none like him, well in Lambert anyway.

# Chapter Eleven

That is basically our town, there are people that come and go, there are city folk who decide to move up for something different, but all in all it's just the few people, that make up Lambert. The city folk never stay very long. They get bored and move on. They don't have much patience. The only time we ever hear a horn toot is when one of them city folk pulls up behind two cockies chatting from their cars in Main Street. Most people around here just get out their car and go join the conversation, but the city folk, they don't want to stop, they gotta be somewhere. I don't know where, as there really isn't much to do around here but sit in your car and chat to your neighbour. I mean don't get me wrong we have our exciting moments. Like the time Old Bill took his son out shooting rabbits and when Pete had to chase that damned pig.

Oh, old Bill taking his son shooting, that was a right laugh. I don't reckon Jimmy has run so fast in all his life. His fat little legs were almost on fire they were chaffing so hard down that hill. You see old Bill had taken his Jimmy out shooting trying to make a man of him, he was a bit girly, would prefer to sit and draw than go out and play with sticks and stuff. Some say that when Old Bill and Beryl went out, Jimmy would sneak into their room and try on his mother's clothes, although that is just a rumour, no one knows for sure. But anyway on this day, Bill had taken Jimmy up over the big hill just outside of town; they had gone on the horses as do many people in these parts.

The sun was shining, the birds were singing and we could heart the distant pops of the rifle. We all sat outside in the beer garden out the front of the pub, truth is, it's not really a beer garden, its just a bench seat with a pot plant next to it. But we were sitting there when we hear this God awful high pitched scream coming down the hill.

"Bloody wild boars" Pete said lazily, as he sipped his beer.

"Not a pig there Pete, that's young Jimmy" Joe replied looking up the hill.

Pete looked over to see Jimmy, head down, running as fast as he could, his mouth pulled back in a grimace, his blonde hair wet with sweat, tears streaming down his face.

"Aw heck, I hope Bill's alright" Pete said, as we all began to run toward Jimmy to find out what the screaming was about.

"I killed me old man" Jimmy panted as he collapsed on the road in a sobbing mess.

Pete and Joe ran for the tractor ute. It wasn't long before they were coming back, Pete and Joe, tears were cascading down their faces. Old Bill was laid out in the back of the tray.

"What the hell happened Pete?" I said, looking at Bill's face, who was obviously not dead, but had blood smeared up the side of his cheeks.

Pete and Joe laughed so hard, they could barely climb out the ute. Joe held his stomach, his eyes squinted and tears fell from the corners.

"He was..." Pete said not able to get out the rest.

Bernie and I looked at each other confused; Jimmy sat on the ground with his head between his knees, his cheeks dirty and streaked with tears.

"Jimmy what happened mate?" Bernie said, as she clamoured her way down to the ground.

"Well, me dad and me were our shootin' rabbits and I got one right?" Bernie nodded as I sat down on the other side of Jimmy to hear the story.

"And well I shot the rabbit and dad reckons I gotta gut the bugger, so I gut it but when I flicked me knife out the bloody guts come right off the knife and wrapped itself right round 'is neck"

Pete and Joe laughed hysterically, Bernie shot them a murderous look, but there was no stopping them.

"'Is face went blue 'ey and I fort I killed 'im, is he alright?" Jimmy said.

We could hear a cough and splutter from the back of the ute and went to look to see old Bill trying to sit up.

"Jimmy" he called.

"Yeah dad I'm 'ere" Jimmy called, climbing up into the back of the ute.

Bill sat up and looked at him; Jimmy sat and smiled at his dad as relief flooded his face. Bill reached up and cracked Jimmy in the back of his head, the loud thud made us all wince.

"You're a bloody idiot Jimmy, a bloody idiot, you coulda friggin' killed me then" Bill said.

Jimmy dropped his head, tears prickled at his eyes. Needless to say that never did Old Bill take Jimmy shooting again. Last I heard Jimmy had moved to the city and was some sort of entertainer. Old Bill just says that he did something wrong with that boy, just didn't know what. That was a funny day, but so was the day that the pig got out.

# Chapter Twelve

The pig was squealin', screaming like I've never heard before. Blue was on one side, Pete on the other, and me coming up the flank, we were on the run. The grass rushed past us so fast I was beginning to think there was going to be a grass fire. Sweat ran down our faces. I looked over at Blue, whose face was red; flies didn't even have time to stick to his back he was moving so fast. He twisted and turned, just when we thought we had the pig, he'd be off again. But this time we had him, he was slowing down, his pace wasn't as quick anymore.

"Get 'im Blue" Pete yelled.

Blue put his head down, his arms moved faster, his blue jeans and boots a blur, his legs were like a well-stocked steam train and he was on top of the pig. His shadow covered the pink little body of the squealer. Blue leapt into the air, arms spread like an eagle soaring high, his legs sprawled out behind him, slowly and not so gracefully he came crashing down like a fat kid doing a belly flop at the pool. I could hear Blue gasp for air and then we heard that familiar high pitched squeal, we looked up the hill and watched the fat pink bum and tail take off.

"Bloody thing" Blue snarled as he stood up and dusted the grass from his jeans. "Ripped me favourites too ma, was gonna wear these down the pub an' all" he complained as he poked at the hole in his jeans.

Pete and I looked up to see if the pig had come to a stop. But I reckon he went up over the hill and became wild dog food.

Rosalita our old sow had, had piglets, ten of the flamin' things. Still not sure how she managed to get pregnant in the first place, seeing as there hasn't been a boar around here. I'm still waiting for an answer from Matt and John as to how it happened, as they often liked to take her for a walk and I'm wondering if that walk included going past Macca's boars. But keeping the damned piglets in the pen was a right chore. That little piglet was the biggest of escape artists. He knew the cracks, we'd fix one hole and there the next morning he'd be eating my carrots. The last straw came when Pete came out one morning and there it was eating his prize winning tomatoes.

"That's it, we're 'aving pork for tea tonight" Pete roared.

Blue and I came out into the morning light, looking over the veggie patch to see a little pink backside sticking up out of the lettuce. He looked up almost smiling, he was so proud of his escapee techniques; his face was stained red with tomato juice. Pete's face red even under his whiskers, but his face was red from anger not tomatoes.

"Want ya gun dad?" Blue asked, looking at his father.

"Nup, gonna catch it and break it's friggin' neck" Pete said slowly walking down towards the pig.

No sooner had Pete got three steps away and it was off. Pete close behind, his slippers flapping around on his feet. He stopped and threw them high across the yard. I saw one hurtle towards my head and swiftly dodged the moccasin missile. Blue, quickly grabbed Pete's gumboots and ran after his father, handing them to him. Pete didn't even stop, he hopped on one foot, while he put a boot on the other, falling into a pile of cow manure that I hadn't had a chance to dig in yet. I winced as he stood up, his freshly cleaned and ironed flannelette shirt covered in brown sludge and hay. He wiped his hands on his jeans and hurdled the back gate, as he ran through the sheep the piglet squealed all the way to the big hill.

The kookaburra's laughed at the sight they could see. Finally I thought I better go join them as the piglet lead Pete and Blue on the chase of their life. Dodging sheep, tree's, Fanny Mabel and both men. I grabbed some bread and tomatoes out of the kitchen and pulled on my boots.

"Pig, pig, pig" I called and waved the bag.

I watched the pig turn quickly and come towards me, which caused Pete and Blue who were running either side of it nearly collide. And there we spent the morning chasing the pig that got away. We heard sightings of it all afternoon, but we knew better than to tell Pete who was out back holding a funeral for his fallen tomatoes. They were brave tomatoes, taken far too early, by a savage enemy; a pig.

# Chapter Thirteen

Did I tell you how I met my Pete? Well that is a right yarn. You see Pete was a city bloke. Believe it or not. As much as I say harsh things about the city folk, we do on occasions get some that stay and end up more country than the dry bare fields themselves. And Pete was one of them city folks.

You see it happened when I had turned fifteen; the big ute muster was on. My best friend Lizzie and I desperately wanted to go, but knew our mum and dad wouldn't let us go, so we made up some cock and bull story about going to each other's house or camping or something like that. I don't remember the details now. But the Saturday night came; we thumbed our way out to the big field just outside of town. Simmo owned the land, he was one of those strange blokes that lived on his own, he owned a mechanic shop in town, it's not there now, but we were always taught you never go into the toilet at his shop because he had cameras. Don't know whether that was true or not, but you were always cautious anyway.

So a thunderstorm was coming in fast, the smell of rain was in the air; we jumped off the back of the ute of some bloke and his missus that had picked us up on the way. We found a prime spot under a big gum, the grass a small patch of green, soon to be flattened by our tent. We were sitting in the small fold out chairs, watching the cowboys in their hotted up V8 utes, the mud flaps flicking mud high into the sky, as they did circle work in the middle of the field, cutting up big round ditches of mud.

Suddenly we heard the rumble of a big V8 pull up next to us, music pounded from the stereo and thudded deep into our chests. We turned to see a green sandman panel van trembling under the weight of the engine. The windows tinted a dark navy blue, the shiny bull bar glistened in the speckled sun that poked through the darkening clouds, the claps of thunder met the revs of the engine. Slowly the panel van passed us, the words sandman painted in yellow and red on the back doors, a small sticker in the window which read "don't laugh your daughter may be in here"

Lizzie and I tried to peek into the car, to see the bloke that would be driving such a beauty. As the car came to a stop and the engine died, the anticipation rose. The door slowly opened and there stood a sight. His blue jeans tight and his flannelette shirt tucked in, just as tightly. His hair blonde, business in the front, party at the back, his arm bulging with a packet of Winnie Blues. I felt my heart skip a beat. I knew that this was the man for me. He reached back into the car and I near fell off me chair as this perfectly rounded bottom bent over in front of us. Lizzie and I swooned and fanned our faces with lust. As he stood back up we could see what he had reached into his car for. We burst into fits of laughter. There he stood as cool as ice, perched on top of his head, a brand new crisp and shiny akubra.

"City bloke" Lizzie and I chorused as he swaggered over in our direction.

"Hi girls, do ya mind if I camp out here in the van next to ya?" He asked.

His voice was so deep and creamy, I was in love.

"Yeah that'd be alright I reckon" I said as I tried to hide the melting that was happening inside.

"Me name's Pete Mollop, I'm not from round here, but it looks like it's gonna be a great turnout hey?"

Lizzie and I nodded in agreement, lost for words. He spent the evening chatting to us about the city and how much he would love to live in the country and how he wants to buy a farm. It was during this conversation and a few too many sips of beer that the wind picked up; the storm had started to get bigger. The cracks of thunder were louder and the lightening lit up the night sky. Suddenly we heard a boom and then a crack and looked up to see the tree that our tent was under split in two. One half falling on top of our tent, the other onto the bare space behind it. Lizzie and I screamed and ran into Pete's arms for protection. Pete grinned like Casanova himself. He still says to this day that even God couldn't have planned that better. So there we stood no tent, nowhere to sleep, our change of clothes, everything hidden underneath an old smouldering gum tree.

"Well girls, I guess I'm gonna be real warm tonight hey?" he said as he grinned, his teeth a perfect white.

Lizzie and I swooned again as we climbed up into the back of Pete's panel van. During the night I would wake occasionally, to feel Pete's arm around my waist, I would wriggle away to have him tighten his arm and pull me closer. It didn't help the melting. The next day we had Pete drop us off a little outside of town, so as not to be caught by any of the local busy bodies. Lizzie jumped out and waited for me at the front of the car, but as I went to get out, Pete grabbed my arm.

"Can I have your number?" he said.

I smiled shyly; I took his hand and the pen he held out for me. I quickly scribbled my phone number down onto the back of his hand. He leaned in and kissed me softly on the corner of my mouth. My face went as red as a tomato as I got out of the car. I ran up to Lizzie unable to wait to tell her what happened and there we stood as Pete drove off, his car rambling up the road. We squealed and jumped up and down, with excitement of our night out. As we walked home we talked speedily getting our stories straight so as not to let anyone on about what had happened.

Now before I go on, let me tell you about Lizzie. She wasn't the type of girl to miss out on the guy, so although she was excited for me, she was jealous as hell. You see Lizzie was the type of girl that always gets what she wanted that was until one particular day. Lizzie had the biggest crush on Smithy, remember the oaf from the pub that Bernie marched out. Well one night at the pub she sauntered around the pool table, gazing lovingly at Smithy as he played pool against some of the local boys. After Smithy had taken his shot, Lizzie smoothed her way in close, running her fingers up his arm.

"What's that? You want to get me another beer?" Smithy looked at her and winked, the twinkle in his eye dancing with amusement.

Lizzie huffed and bustled her way to the bar. As she came back, she noticed an awkward guy standing against the front door, his shoes pointed sharp, his suit dark and suave. His hair was slicked back, we hadn't seen him before, but Lizzie figured he was one of the city folk here. She gave him a sly smile, as she noticed him staring at her almost exposed breasts. His face turned red as he returned her smile, in a sly way, looking over at Smithy to make sure he hadn't seen. Lizzie continued her march over to where Smithy stood and banged his glass of beer down on the table.

"Oi, careful, yer gonna knock the head orf" he said.

Lizzie folded her arms and turned her back, she could see that the city bloke was still watching her every move. She smiled at him again, giving him a little wave. Once again the blokes face turned red and he shifted uncomfortably. Lizzie turned back to Smithy, when she heard him jibing one of the guys that he was playing pool against, she ran her hands up his back.

"Yer gonna jinx me woman, isn't there a table or somethin' you can clean?" he snapped.

Lizzie turned and gave him a quick kick in the shins before stomping back to the bar. She ordered two more beers and turned to face the man standing in the corner.

"Hey you want one of these?" she said as she raised glass.

He nodded and gave a quick glance to Smithy, who didn't even seem to notice what was going on. She sidled up to the guy and whispered into his ear. Smithy had even noticed that Lizzie walked out hand and hand with the guy, leaving the two untouched beers on the table next to the door. Turns out she quickly forgot Smithy that night, but the next morning when she rolled over for a morning cuddle, the bloke was gone and on her bedside table was the unused condom she thought they'd used. She's now got a beautiful little girl, but no city slicker or Smithy. But that's enough about Lizzie; you see I figured Pete wasn't going to ring me. I had heard about these city folk and their ways of one night stands and stuff. Not that we did what one night stands technically mean, but you get what I mean. So you can imagine my surprise when the phone was buzzing its head off in the hall that same day, as I ran for it, beating Sharon, only by a pull of the pony tail. I heard the beeps; the same that would come when various Aunts who lived in Gympie rang.

"Hullo?" I said, expecting to hear the familiar voice of my Aunt Mildred bark down the line.

"Hey do you remember me?" I heard that some deep chocolatey voice of earlier that morning.

"Yeah of course I do" I whispered, my hand over the mouthpiece as Sharon stood next to me desperately trying to listen to the conversation.

"Is that Mildred?" Mum called out.

"No it's a boooooyyyyy" Sharon chanted. Mum looked at me and then at Sharon, who giggled behind her hand. Mum dragged Sharon out of the hall way and into the kitchen. But I knew that they would be standing behind the door still listening. I sighed and went back to the conversation.

"Sorry that was my mum"

"It's ok, hey I was thinking about comin' up next weekend to look at the price of property, wanna come help me look?" Pete asked down the line.

My heart skipped a beat and butterflies danced in my belly; he wanted to see me again. I cleared my throat and shuffled my feet.

"Um sure" I said.

"Alright well where can I meet ya?"

"At the pub, what time?" I asked. I felt the pub would be a safe neutral ground; I didn't want to inflict my family on the poor soul too early.

"Say about ten?"

We said our goodbyes and hung up the phone, as I turned around I saw mum and Sharon looking at me.

"Well?" Mum said.

"What?" I replied, my face reddening as I shrugged my shoulders.

"Well tell me about him" Mum's grin grew to almost take over her whole face; it was worrying how much teeth she could show.

I sighed; I knew that I wasn't going to get out of this one easily. I hadn't been prepared for what to tell her, where I had met him, who he was. How was I going to tell my mum that he was some city bloke who I met at a place I wasn't supposed to be and ended up sleeping in the back of his panel curled up against his chest with my best friend on the other side of him because a tree crushed our tent.

"His name is Pete, I met him down the street, he is from the city, he is coming up here to look at moving up and he is eighteen years old" I said, hoping my lie about where I met him would be convincing.

Mum and Sharon made and ooh noise as I wandered dreamily off to my room, to practice writing my name with his surname over and over in my diary. Well the next weekend came round, not fast enough I reckon, it felt like it took half a year to get here.

# Chapter Fourteen

I didn't tell mum that I was meeting him, because I knew without a doubt they would be following me, hiding behind tree's, bushes and horses so I didn't see them just to get a look. I sat on the front step of the pub; I could hear the distant rumble of a familiar V8 and looked up to see that same green Sandman panel van slowly make its way up to where I sat. It came to an idle in front of the main bar. I stood up and tried to look as cool and calm as I could be, but knew that I was failing as my knees were knocking up a right storm. Pete stepped out of the car, that brand new akubra still perched on top of his head, crisp and shiny.

"Hey" he said touching my cheek.

I smiled up at him and took the akubra off his head.

"If yer gonna be a country bloke we need to fix this first" I grinned.

He smiled at me and cocked his head to one side, a look that still makes me weak at the knees today. I walked over to the back of the car and stuck the akubra under the back tyre.

"Alright now back out" I called as he jumped into the car; he knew what he had to do.

The engine came to a loud roar and there we stood in the middle of Main Street, reversing and driving over his akubra until it was dusty, flat and blackened from the tyres. I picked up the hat and leaned into the window, placing it on his head. He leaned over and patted the passenger seat.

"Gonna come check out this farm I saw in the paper?" he asked.

I nodded and ran around to the front passenger side, buckling my seat belt as we shot off down the road, his hand on my knee to look at what would become our future family home. The home we were to raise three boys and grow old in. A home that one day I would watch slip away, as I closed my eyes for the final time.

Well as I said, Pete bought that farm and he moved up the following weekend. He lived out of the pub for three months waiting for the old cocky who owned it to move out. The farm already came with sixteen hundred head of sheep and thirty cattle. But you know something; city blokes are a bit slow. It took him ages to learn what to do on the farm. But that first weekend after he moved to Lambert, my mum reckoned we should have Pete over for dinner. It was going to be the first time that my parents ever met or even saw him. Dad was already not happy about the fact that his daughter was seeing a city bloke, let alone one that was three years older and drove a car. I didn't have the heart to tell him that it was a shaggin' wagon. So when Pete and I pulled up Saturday night; after a day of moving stuff into the closet they have for rooms at the pub, there Dad sat on the front veranda, his arms folded, his glasses pushed down to the end of his nose, his forehead creased.

"Dad this is Pete, Pete this is me Dad, Ernie" I said as we walked towards the front door.

"G'day" Pete said as he held his hand out to my Dad.

Dad just looked down at his hand and grunted as he got up and walked inside. Pete looked at me bewildered. I shrugged my shoulders, no idea what Dad's problem was. Mum on the other hand came running out of the kitchen as she wiped her hands on her apron and squealed with delight. She held her arms out and wrapped them around Pete, resting her head on his chest.

"Welcome to the family luv" she said.

I looked at her with a murderous look in my eye.

"Mum" I said through gritted teeth.

"Oh don't mind her, she just can't see what I do" mum said taking Pete's hand and leading him into the lounge room.

I sighed and followed, then stopped dead in the doorway when I saw my dad sitting in his favourite high back brown armchair, polishing his shotgun.

"Dad what are you doing?" I said, mortified.

Dad looked up and continued to polish.

"I just want to get to know your young boyfriend here, off you go and help yer mother in the kitchen" he said evilly.

I looked at Pete and mouth the word sorry. He smiled and waved me out the door.

"Mum do you know what Dad is doing?" I said as I walked into the kitchen.

"Yes luv I do, he is trying to find out Pete's intentions" she said as she busied herself with the roast.

"Couldn't he do it without the gun?" I asked shaking my head. My family was nuts. Have I mentioned that?

Mum just laughed. Later that evening throughout dinner, Pete was deathly silent, he didn't talk much and it wasn't until two weeks later I found out what my dad said to Pete. There he had sat polishing that gun and with a low deep voice not even looking at Pete he begun to speak.

"You know I love my daughter dearly and I love the fact that she has found a bloke that makes her happy. But I tell you somethin' else, I'm also an excellent shot and you do anythin' to hurt my girl and I will make sure that your testicles are no longer. And another thing, get rid of that sin bin of a car you have. Buy a ute, your flamin' country now, not some city bloke."

I asked Pete what he did. He told me that all he could do was sit there and say yes sir. But the next day he went out and put a deposit on a rusted out red ute that coughed and sputtered down the road. Luckily for Pete, one thing he could do was fix a car blindfolded. I guess that's where Blue got his abilities. But Dad soon grew to love Pete, he realised that he was a top bloke, even if he was a bit slow in learning how to work a farm. But I was there to help and I made sure to help him keep his head above water. I taught him to dip and drench, to crutch, to talk to the shearers and ringers, to muster and to shoot a gun. After a while he became as country as a blowie, but it sure did make for some funny stories in the process.

# Chapter Fifteen

One of the funniest stories that Pete and I share is the first time I took him shooting. We were hunting roo's; we had shot a big male and had it slung up in the back of the ute. Pete stood against the ute with a grin spread across his face as he gloated about his catch, stunned that he didn't fall over when the rifle went off. Suddenly I saw movement behind him, at first I thought it was the kangaroo coming back to life, but then I watched as a big black head reared up behind Pete's shoulder. It's red belly shining bright, warning of danger. I held up the rifle, pointed it just slightly left of Pete's ear, his face suddenly drained of all colour and his grin turned into a grimace of sheer terror. I reckon that if all had been quiet I would have heard his balls knocking against his knee caps. I pulled the trigger and heard the crack. Pete screamed, running to the front of the ute.

"What the hell are you doin'?" he screamed at me, his face red and contorted in anger.

I simply pointed at the back of the ute and there on the top of the opened hale bale was a huge red bellied black snake, missing a head. I can't really say what he said, but let's just say, if it were TV there would be plenty of bleeps.

"Why couldn't ya just tell me to move?" he squealed, his once deep voice now a few octaves higher.

"Well I dunno I just went with the flow" I said with a shrug.

"With the flow? With the flow? You near took me flamin' head orf" he screamed, his face red, his eyes still bulging and the veins throbbing in his temples. It was the first argument we had ever had.

"Well yer not dead are ya? Ya big girl, come on man up and get over it, the snake didn't bite ya, I didn't shoot ya, stop being a sook" I yelled back.

It was then that the hysterical laughter took over; I couldn't hold it back anymore. There I stood, tears streaming down me face, Pete stood there with his hands on his hips, his face red, his forehead creased.

"You shoulda seen yer face. Mate." I said imitating his look of shock.

Finally he began to see the funny side of what had just happened and there we stood, the sun setting pink and red, the wind sweeping the grass around our ankles, a dead roo and snake in the back of the ute. Pete and I folded over each other we laughed so hard we almost pee'd. Even the kookaburras joined us. It was a story we have told and retold to our kids, our kids friends and all the city folk that come to visit the pub, of course if you ask Pete, I skinned his ear and the snake was big enough to eat a small baby. But then you ask Pete about mozzies and he reckons they could off with ya family dog. He likes to tell the tall tale here and there. But I love him all the same, he's me man and I wouldn't give him up for any other.

He got used to the country pretty quick and the locals got used to him quick too. I remember he asked me to marry him when we were on a date at the pub. I know what you're thinking it wasn't a romantic place to go on a date, but to be honest there really isn't anywhere else to go around here. But he cleared his voice, tapped his glass and got everyone's attention. Slowly he climbed down off his stool and knelt in front of me. Out of his pocket he pulled my mum's engagement ring, remember we were young and didn't have a lot of money, and we certainly don't have a jewellers in town, so any ring would have made me happy, hell he could have used a ring pull off the can of beer and I would have been thrilled. Well there on one knee in the pub, everyone looking on, Bernie and Joe, had just taken it over at that time; Bernie stood looking on swooning with delight, mum let out a squeal of excitement, Pete asked me to marry him. Well let's face it how could a girl say no to him? With those dimples, baby blues and a smile that makes your knees weak.

Our wedding had virtually the whole town attend. I didn't want a big fancy wedding in the church; I've always felt more at home out on the land. Luckily for us at the very bottom of our property runs a small creek, shaded by willow trees and I had decided with mum of course, that this would be the perfect place to be married. Mrs Miller made me a special dress to wear, she even held back on the sequins. Sharon and Morrie were my bridesmaids and we had Lauren and Janelle as flower girls. Mum took on all the catering and decorating. I couldn't wait to be Pete's wife. I was never a girl to dream about my wedding, but what I got was perfect.

Mum had borrowed a length of white fabric from Mrs Miller and laid it down under the willow tree. Pete and Dad had organised a bunch of chairs from the church to be sat down beside the creek. I couldn't hold the tears back as Dad walked me down the freshly mowed path to the willow tree. Mum stood there beaming with pride. She pulled back the willow leaves and looked to see Pete standing looking dapper in a dark suit and a single tear running down his cheek. Sharon grinned at me and

Morrie dabbed his eyes with a tissue, while Dale stood looking ever handsome as Pete's best man.

The service wasn't very long as Rev. Patrick was pretty drunk and couldn't remember the words. But none of that mattered to me; I was marrying the man of my dreams. I was going to live the rest of my days with not only my best mate, but my soul mate. It was one of the happiest days of my life. The other happiest days were when Blue, Matt and John were born. After we said I do and Pete bent forward to give me our first kiss as husband and wife the party started. Mum with the help of the C.W.A ladies pulled out endless supplies of pot roast, casseroles, pies and salads. There was plenty of beer flowing, the band which consisted of a few kids that could play guitar played some Slim Dusty and Johnny Cash songs.

Every year Pete and I on our anniversary visit our tree, which he carved our names into and we spend the day down there. We also manage to sneak in a few kisses and cuddles, in fact, don't tell the boys but each of them was conceived under that tree. But I won't get into too many details there.

So that is pretty much Lambert, our little town. It's a nice spot, quiet and nestled away in the hills. It's not busy like the city, but that's the way I like it. So now you know most of the people that are here, well the ones that have a worthy story to tell, I reckon everyone has a story to tell, just some aren't worth listening to. But there is someone I left till last to introduce you to and that's me. My name is Molly Alice Rose Mollop. I am forty three years old, married to the most wonderful man to grace this earth. We have three handsome young men. And speaking of my boys, I bet you are wondering what happened to that old Jersey cow, Fanny Mabel, well I got a phone call just this morning.

# Chapter Sixteen

The phone was buzzing madly, so I raced in from the veggie patch, it was old Mrs Barker on the line, she is our neighbour; grumpy old bat she is too. You know one thing I really don't like about Lambert is the town is so damned small you can't pick your neighbours. But anyway she tells me that she has my cow.

"Matt, John, come in here please" I called out to the boys, who were busy riding their bikes round and round in circles out in the yard.

I watched as they sauntered into the kitchen, sitting down at the table, the looked at each other, they knew that they were in trouble, but not sure for what

"Mrs Barker just rang" I said, their faces became full of recognition. "Why is Fanny Mabel at her place, eating her price winning roses?"

Matt and John began to giggle, I cleared my throat and they both snapped into silence.

"Well she took our footy and when we asked for it back she said we couldn't have it" Matt said.

"And so we took her garden gnome and held it for ransom, but she still wouldn't give the footy back, even when we cut its head off and left it on the front door step" Matt gave John a quick jab in the ribs, as John had given away too much in his confession.

I raised my eyebrow, as I tried to stifle my giggles at the thought of how the old bat would have reacted to finding the decapitated head of her garden gnome that she had named Elfie on the doorstep.

"So you thought you would take Fanny Mabel down to eat her pride and joy?" I said sternly.

"Yeah that's right" Matt said, while John nodded excessively.

"And did she give you back the footy?" I asked.

"Well no not yet, cause she rang ya and we haven't been back, ya reckon she'll give it to us now?" John asked.

"Well as a matter of fact I know she will because she told that if you come and get the cow she will have put the footy on the letterbox for you" I answered.

Matt and John high fived each other and waltzed out the back door to Mrs Barkers house to get Fanny Mabel. Which is a good thing because my lawns really need a mow. We would have a mower but Blue took that and dismantled it to put a motor on the wheelbarrow, just to make it better. You know I'm really glad though that you have come and shared this story with me and I hope when you are travelling on through Lambert that you will stop in and say g'day and have a cuppa. But I've gotta get the tea on, Pete will be home from a long week in the truck and the boys will no doubt be home with Fanny Mabel soon and as usual they will be famished. But like we like to say in the bush, this isn't goodbye, its just seeya next time I'm lookin' at ya.

# Don't miss out!

Visit the website below and you can sign up to receive emails whenever Davis McAlonan publishes a new book. There's no charge and no obligation.

https://books2read.com/r/B-A-IYBV-QGEBC

**BOOKS 2 READ**

Connecting independent readers to independent writers.

# Also by Davis McAlonan

The Mollops

# About the Author

Davis McAlonana is an Australian author who loves to make people laugh. Their stories are filled with emotion and humor. All of Davis McAlonan's work targets young adults and those who prefer clean romance.

www.ingramcontent.com/pod-product-compliance
Lightning Source LLC
Chambersburg PA
CBHW061635130726

47996CB00003B/1286